P9-AOI-666

-My Family-

My Grandparents

by Claudia Harrington
illustrated by Zoe Persico

Looking Glass Library

An Imprint of Magic Wagon
abdopublishing.com

To my amazing family, with additional thanks to Nabra Nelson. —CH

To my grandparents for loving me as much as they do and fueling me with delicious Italian meals. —ZP

abdopublishing.com

Published by Magic Wagon, a division of ABDO, PO Box 398166, Minneapolis, Minnesota 55439. Copyright © 2016 by Abdo Consulting Group, Inc. International copyrights reserved in all countries. No part of this book may be reproduced in any form without written permission from the publisher. Looking Glass Library™ is a trademark and logo of Magic Wagon.

Printed in the United States of America, North Mankato, Minnesota.
052015
092015

THIS BOOK CONTAINS
RECYCLED MATERIALS

Written by Claudia Harrington
Illustrated by Zoe Persico
Edited by Heidi M.D. Elston
Designed by Candice Keimig

Library of Congress Cataloging-in-Publication Data

Harrington, Claudia, 1957- author.
    My grandparents / by Claudia Harrington ; illustrated by Zoe Persico.
        pages cm. -- (My family)
    Summary: Lenny follows Layla for a school project and learns what it is like to live with grandparents.
    ISBN 978-1-62402-105-3
1. Grandparents--Juvenile fiction. 2. Grandparent and child--Juvenile fiction. 3. Families--Juvenile fiction. [1. Grandparents--Fiction. 2. Grandparent and child--Fiction. 3. Family life--Fiction. 4. Youths' art.]
I. Persico, Zoe, 1993- illustrator. II. Title.
PZ7.1.H374Mn 2016
[E]--dc23
                                    2015002664

"Good morning, second graders!" said
Miss Fish.

"Good morning," said the class.

"Lenny," said Miss Fish, "Principal Baccus needs to see you."

"Oooooooh!" said the class.

Lenny's face burned.

Miss Fish smiled. "Layla, please go with Lenny."

Layla ran up to Principal Baccus. "Grampa!"

"Your grandfather's the principal?" asked Lenny.

Principal Baccus hugged Layla, then turned to Lenny. "You'll be coming to our house today. Layla is Student of the Week."

Lenny let out a sigh and slid into a chair.

They all laughed.

"Back to class, kids," said Principal Baccus.

"See you later, Lenny."

When the final bell rang, Lenny got
the class camera from Miss Fish.
"Here you go, Ace Reporter," she said.
Layla posed for Lenny. **Click!**

"How do you get home?" Lenny asked Layla.

"It's a surprise!" said Layla with a wink.

Layla ran down the front steps into a big grandmother hug.
"Cool!" said Lenny, eyeing the bikes they would be riding.

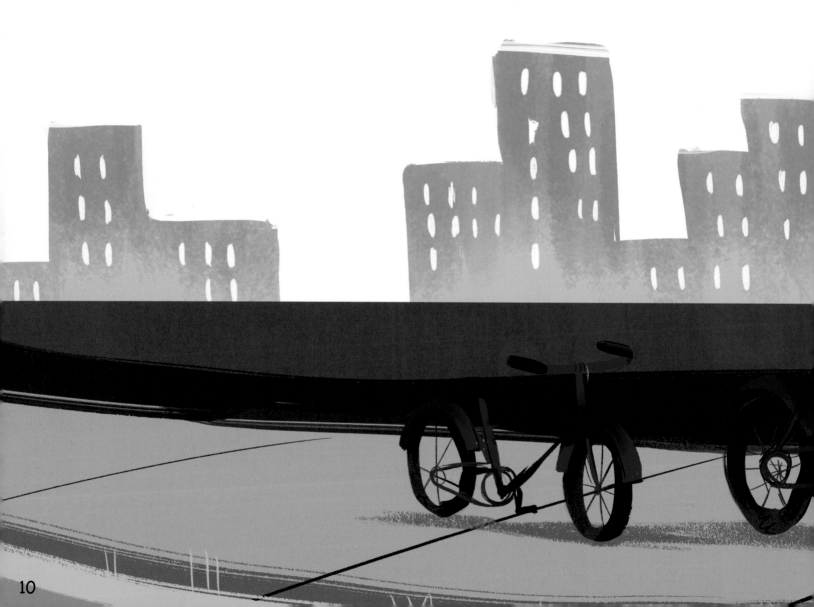

"We brought an extra helmet for you, Lenny," said Layla. "This is my Grams. And this is Petunia." Layla gave her dog a quick kiss.

"Nice to meet you," said Lenny.

"My pleasure," said Grams.

"Ready for blastoff?"

"Almost," said Lenny. **Click!**

When they got home, they put away the bikes.
Grams asked, "Any science homework?"
"NO HOMEWORK TONIGHT!" Lenny and
Layla shouted together.

"How about a snack?" asked Grams.
"Can we have some astronaut ice cream?" asked Layla.
"Before dinner?" Grams opened the cupboard. "Only if you don't tell your grandfather!"

Lenny smiled. "Would you get sent to the principal's office if he finds out?"

"We'd just have to bring him some." Layla laughed.

"What flavor do you want?
Neapolitan or mint chip?" asked Layla.

Lenny scrunched up his mouth. "Is your grams going to bake cookies? I shouldn't have both." Layla howled. "Grams? Bake?"
"Errr, mint chip," said Lenny. **Click!**

"Yum," said Lenny. "So who makes
your dinner?"
"Grampa," said Layla between bites.

"Did I hear my name?" asked Grampa.

"Lenny! Nice to see you again.

Meet Layla's sisters, Abby and Dana."

Click!

"Come on! Let me show you our telescope," said Layla.

"Wow! Who taught you what to look for?" asked Lenny.

"Grams," said Layla. "She used to be an astronaut."

"Hey! I think I see a UFO!" said Lenny.

"Let me see," said Layla. **Click!**

When Layla peered in, she shook with laughter.

"That's not a UFO, Lenny. It's a Frisbee! Abby, Dana, knock it off!"

Layla's sisters giggled from behind a bush. **Click!**

21

"Can you see any real stuff in there?" asked Lenny.

"Sure," said Layla. "Look at the moon's craters. That lower one's Tycho."

"Cool! Who taught you their names?" asked Lenny.

"Grams," Layla said.

"Calling all astronauts," said Grampa. "Dinner!"
"Grampa makes the best kabobs and hummus. Usually he lets me wash the veggies!" said Layla. **Click!**

When they finished eating, Layla pulled Lenny from the floor. "Come see my room!"

"Stellar!" said Lenny. "You get to have a trampoline in your room?"

Layla nodded. "I sometimes pretend it's zero gravity at bedtime."

24

"Check this out, Lenny," said Layla, turning off her lights. Her ceiling glowed brightly.

"Awesome!" oohed Lenny. **Click!**

"Does Petunia sleep with you?" asked Lenny.

"Yes," said Layla, bouncing on the trampoline, "if I don't launch myself into space—" **Click!**

"Then her grandmother reads her books about women space pioneers," said Grams. Grampa added, "And her grandfather tells her about the times *he* got sent to the principal's office." Lenny's eyes bugged out. They all laughed.

Lenny's mom poked her head in. "Am I late?"

"You missed the last rocket to Mars," said Lenny. "But I have one more question for the *Star* of the Week. Who loves you best?"

"We do!" said Layla's grandparents together.
Click!

"And I love *you* best," said Lenny's mom.

"Time to go," she said.

Student of the Week

Layla

Lenny waved good-bye. "See you around the planet, astro-nut."

Layla grinned. "Tomorrow, moon man!"

WITHDRAWN